~The~
BEST KIND
of GIFT

Kathi Appelt

illustrated by

Paul Brett Johnson

HarperCollins Publishers

To Elizabeth Harper Neeld
and in honor of
Reverend Tommy and Miss Rachel Harper
Amen!

—K.A.

For Ben, Chris, Sarah, and Bob Rathbone

with additional thanks to Ellen, Doug, and Keith

—P.B.J.

The Best Kind of Gift   Text copyright © 2003 by Kathi Appelt
Illustrations copyright © 2003 by Paul Brett Johnson
Manufactured in China. All rights reserved.   www.harperchildrens.com

Library of Congress Cataloging-in-Publication Data   Appelt, Kathi, date.
The best kind of gift / by Kathi Appelt ; illustrated by Paul Brett Johnson.   p.   cm.
Summary: Jory fears that he is too small to find a suitable gift to welcome the new parson.
ISBN 0-688-15392-5 — ISBN 0-688-15393-3 (lib. bdg.)
[1. Size—Fiction.   2. Gifts—Fiction.]   I. Johnson, Paul Brett, ill.   II. Title.
PZ7.A6455 Be   2003   [Fic]—dc21   2001024751

Typography by Carla Weise
1 2 3 4 5 6 7 8 9 10
❖
First Edition

Yes, indeed!

There was a brand-new parson at the Dogwood All-Faiths Tabernacle—Brother Harper. He'd come all the way from Nashville on his mule, Old Faithful, to lead the congregation. Folks in Dogwood were mighty pleased to have him, so right away they decided to have a pounding.

But little Jory Timmons, he was so small, he didn't even know what a pounding was.

"It's when everyone takes *a pound o' this and a pound o' that* to help make Brother Harper feel at home," Mama said.

"*Everyone?*" Jory asked.

"Mmm-hmm." Mama nodded. "I'm gonna bake a fresh blackberry pie."

"Is a pie the same as a pound?" asked Jory.

Mamma dabbed his nose with flour. "Not exactly, but a pie is a treat. The best kind of gift is a treat."

A blackberry pie! Could Jory take a blackberry pie to help welcome Brother Harper?

"Oh, sweetie," said Mama, handing him a slice of pie crust, "you need to be a little bit bigger to use the oven."

Jory looked at the big black oven in the corner of the kitchen. He was sure it looked back at him! He shuddered. He felt as small as a corn cake.

But he wanted to take a treat to Brother Harper too. What could it be?

Maybe Papa would know.

"I'm gonna take a pail o' Bessie's good creamy milk," said Papa.

"Is a pail the same as a pound?" Jory asked.

"Not exactly, but that doesn't matter so long as you give it gladly," Papa replied. "The best kind of gift is given gladly."

Well, Jory, he'd gladly milk ol' Bessie if Papa would let him.

"Can I?" he asked.

To Jory's surprise, Papa said, "Well, sure you can, little fella."

Then Papa showed Jory how to squeeze Bessie's udder, beginning with his thumb and forefinger and pulling down. Jory tried it just like Papa showed him, but no matter how hard he squeezed and pulled down, no milk came out.

"Mooooo!" Bessie bellowed.

Papa just laughed and patted Jory on the back. "That's okay, son. I guess you'll just have to get a little bit bigger."

Jory sighed. He felt as small as a barn cat. He wanted to take something to Brother Harper too, but what could he give gladly?

Thomas! Maybe his big brother would know.

"Gonna take a sack of this good corn," Thomas told Jory.

"Is a sack the same as a pound?"

"It's more than a pound, but that doesn't matter so long as it's useful. The best kind of gift is useful."

Jory looked at the golden corn. He knew it would be used to help feed Old Faithful. Heck, the only thing more useful than a mule was the corn to feed it. He asked Thomas if he could take some corn too.

"Can you lift that sack?" Thomas pointed to the full burlap bag. Jory tugged. He strained. But no matter how hard he tried, the sack of corn wouldn't budge.

"Guess you're gonna have to get a little bit bigger," Thomas said.

Jory felt as small as a pigeon. What could such a small boy carry that would be useful too?

Maybe Granny would know.

"Oooh, I'm gonna take a basketful o' fresh eggs," clucked Granny. She was holding her large straw basket in one hand. With the other she gently reached underneath the hens and pulled out their warm, speckled eggs.

Each of Granny's hens had her own special place to roost and her own special name. There were Tillie and Junie and Brunhilda and Priscilla and Marshmallow and Queenie and Donella and all the others. Jory had a hard time telling them apart.

"Is a basket the same as a pound?" Jory asked.

"Oooh, no, but that doesn't matter so long as you're proud of it. The best kind of gift is one you're proud to give."

Jory would definitely be proud to take some of Granny's special eggs to Brother Harper.

He tiptoed up to Queenie, but when he reached underneath her, he must've reached too fast. Before he knew it, hens were flying everywhere. The air in the henhouse filled up with flapping and feathers.

"Oooh!" exclaimed Granny. She and Jory scrambled out of there as fast as they could.

Granny brushed a feather out of her hair. "Jory," she clucked, "let's wait until you're a little bit bigger for next time."

Jory felt smaller than the smallest June bug. He was too small to bake a pie. Too small to milk a cow. Too small to carry a sack of corn. He was even too small to gather eggs.

Everyone, *everyone* else had something to give to help welcome Brother Harper. The pounding was tomorrow. Jory would never get a little bit bigger in time.

"Shucks!" he said out loud as he walked across the yard. In front of him sat a small flat stone. He kicked it with the toe of his shoe. It bounced a short way. He kicked it again, this time as hard as he could. *Thunk, thunk, thunk.*

"Looks like you've found a mighty good rock there, boy."
Grandpa knelt next to the fence, wrapping a piece of burlap around
the roots of a small apple sapling.

"Is that what you're taking to the pounding?" Jory asked, pointing
to the tree.

"Sure is," Grandpa replied, as he wrapped twine around the bundle
at the bottom of the tree.

"Is a tree the same as a pound?" Jory wondered.

"Nah," replied Grandpa. "But that doesn't matter. It's just something I like. The best kind of gift is one you'd like to get yourself." He finished tying the bundle and looked at Jory. "Now, then, what're you gonna do with that rock?" he asked.

Jory looked at the flat, smooth rock. He picked it up and rubbed it. It was warm from the heat of the afternoon sun. It felt good to hold it. It would feel even better to throw it across the water on the pond and make it skip. He looked up at Grandpa.

Grandpa's eyes twinkled. "Let's go!" he said.

All the way to the pond Jory and Grandpa kept their eyes open for more rocks, the kind that were just so—smooth and flat, not too thick, and no bigger than silver dollars. It was hard work finding them, but Jory was good at it, better even than Grandpa.

Grandpa laughed. "I guess you're just the right size for finding skipping rocks," he said.

For the rest of the afternoon, Jory and Grandpa took turns throwing them across the pond. They had contests to see who could throw the farthest, who could make the biggest splash, and finally who could make a rock skip the greatest number of times. It was an even match, and by the time the sun began to go down, Jory had forgotten all about being small.

But he hadn't forgotten about the pounding.

The next day everyone, *everyone* in Dogwood County showed up at the parsonage to welcome Brother Harper. The house was filled with folks, who brought bags of roasted peanuts, jars of sweet pickles and homemade peach preserves, canned green beans, loaves of bread, pounds o' this and pounds o' that.

When Mama presented her delicious blackberry pie, Brother Harper exclaimed, "What a treat!"

When Papa handed over his pail of cream, along with a pound of freshly ground coffee, Brother Harper shook his hand. "Now these I gladly accept."

Thomas offered his sack of corn, a useful gift for sure. Brother Harper looked inside. "Old Faithful will appreciate this!" he said.

Granny proudly presented her speckled eggs. Brother Harper stated, "I'm proud to have such fine eggs."

Grandpa planted his apple sapling right beside the parsonage's front porch, then stood back and admired it. Brother Harper admired it too.

Finally, it was Jory's turn to present his gift. He walked slowly up to the tall, gentle parson and handed him a brown paper bag.

"What's this?" asked Brother Harper.

"Open it," whispered Jory. Then he added, "It's exactly one pound."

Carefully Brother Harper peered inside the bag. A puzzled look crossed his broad face, and he scratched his head.

Jory looked down at his shoes. Maybe his gift wasn't right at all.

But then a broad smile swept across Brother Harper's face and his eyes twinkled. "Why, I've never seen such good throwing rocks in all my days!" He chuckled. He looked right at Jory. "You must've worked awfully hard to find a whole pound of such perfect rocks."

Jory shook his head. His own smile was as broad as could be.

"Yep," continued Brother Harper, admiring the pile of rocks. "The best kind of gift comes directly from the heart."

Amen!